A Day with Dad

Bo R. Holmberg   illustrated by Eva Eriksson

CANDLEWICK PRESS
CAMBRIDGE, MASSACHUSETTS

Tim waits on the platform at the train station. He's just moved to this town. He lives here with his mom. His dad lives in another town. But today, Tim's dad is coming on the train. They are going to spend the whole day together—just Tim and Dad.

The train pulls into the station and comes to a stop. Then it sighs, as if it's tired from the long journey. Then the door sighs open, too. And there is Dad!

As Mom says, "Good-bye," Dad gives Tim a hug and lifts him into the air.

"Hello, Tim!" he says. "What should we do today?"

Tim knows. He knows what they should do.

At the little stand on Main Street, you can buy hot dogs.

This is where Tim stops.

"Two hot dogs, please," says Dad.

"This is my dad," Tim tells the hot dog lady.

When they finish their hot dogs, Dad says, "Where to now, Tim?"

"Let's see a movie!" says Tim, and he leads Dad to the movie theater. A cartoon movie is showing in five minutes.

"You like cartoons, don't you?" Dad asks.

Tim nods *yes*.

As they enter the theater, Tim hands over the tickets.
The man who tears them has a big mustache. "Dad and
I are going to see this movie," Tim tells him.

Tim and Dad find seats near the middle—Tim always likes to sit in the middle. As they watch the movie, sometimes Dad laughs. He has a funny laugh. When Tim hears Dad laugh, it makes him laugh, too.

When the lights come on, Dad says, "Time for pizza!"

Tim shows Dad his favorite pizza place. It's called
Santana's, and it's not far from the movie theater.
The waiter there lives in Tim's building.

"Hello there, Tim," he says when they walk in.

"Hello," says Tim. "I'm here with my dad."

Dad orders a calzone, and Tim orders a kid's-size pizza.
Both Tim and Dad drink soda. Tim has orange soda and
Dad has root beer.

Tim doesn't eat the crusts but leaves them on his plate in a ring. Dad eats every last crumb and finishes all of his root beer.

"That wasn't bad at all," he says, and takes out his wallet.

"Dad wants to pay!" Tim shouts to his friend the waiter.

When they leave the pizzeria, it's getting dark. Dad looks at his watch. Tim knows that Dad will have to go back soon. But not just yet. Tim knows where they can go.

Tim and Dad sit together in the library. Dad flicks through a magazine while Tim holds a book. He's going to check it out. Tim doesn't know what time it is. He doesn't want to know. He doesn't want Dad's train to leave soon.

The librarian has a ponytail and glasses. Her name is Carol.

"Hello, Tim," she says.

"I'm going to borrow a book," Tim tells her. "Just me. Not Dad." He points at Dad. "This is my dad," he says.

Tim tucks the book under his arm, and they leave together— Tim and Dad.

"Let's have a snack before I go," says Dad.

So Tim and Dad go into a coffee shop nearby. Dad holds Tim up so he can see what's in the case. "I'll have an éclair," says Tim. Dad orders a coffee and cinnamon roll for himself.

When they are done eating, it is late. Dad has to catch his train. As they walk to the station, Dad holds Tim's hand. Dad's hand is big, and Tim's small hand disappears inside it.

When they get to the station, there is still time before the train leaves. "Would you like to see inside the train, Tim?" Dad asks.

"Sure," says Tim.

Dad lifts him up and they climb on board the train.

There are lots of people inside. Everyone is lifting up bags or hanging up coats and jackets.

    "Excuse me," Dad announces to the people in the train car. "Can I say something?"

    Everyone stops and stares at him.

    "Well," Dad says, "this is Tim. He is my son. He is the best son anyone could have."

Then Dad brings Tim back to the platform. He hugs his son very tight. Then he puts him down and rubs his eyes.

"Good-bye, Tim," Dad says. "We'll see each other again real soon."

When Tim's mom arrives, Dad hurries onto the train. Tim stands on the platform with Mom. They see Dad at the window. When the train starts to move, Dad lifts his hand and waves.

Tim waves back. As the train pulls out of the station, Dad's hand gets smaller and smaller.

Tim and Mom watch the train until they can't see it anymore. Even though Tim can't see the train, the tracks are still there. And one day soon, along those tracks, the train will come back. The train will come back with Dad. And Tim will spend another day with Dad.